Fizz the Fireworks Fairy

Join the **Rainbow Magic Reading Challenge!**

Read the story and collect your fairy points to climb the Reading Rainbow at the back of the book.

This book is worth 10 points.

Special thanks to
Kristin Earhart

ORCHARD BOOKS

First published in Great Britain in 2016 by The Watts Publishing Group

1 3 5 7 9 10 8 6 4 2

© 2016 Rainbow Magic Limited.
© 2016 HIT Entertainment Limited.
Illustrations © Orchard Books 2016

HIT entertainment

A CIP catalogue record for this book is available from the British Library.

ISBN 978 1 40834 100 1

Printed and bound in Great Britain by CPI Group (UK) Ltd, Croydon, CR0 4YY

MIX
Paper from
responsible sources
FSC www.fsc.org   FSC® C104740

The paper and board used in this book are made from wood from responsible sources

Orchard Books
An imprint of Hachette Children's Group
Part of The Watts Publishing Group Limited
Carmelite House, 50 Victoria Embankment, London EC4Y 0DZ

An Hachette UK Company
www.hachette.co.uk
www.hachettechildrens.co.uk

Fizz
the Fireworks
Fairy

by Daisy Meadows

ORCHARD

www.rainbowmagic.co.uk

The
Fairyland
Palace

Tat

Woods

Sundown

Main Street

...ottage

Jack Frost's
Ice Castle

Playground

Sundown Lake

Jack Frost's Spell

Everyone loves a good fireworks show,
But I think they're boring places to go.
Some sparklers, some spinners, a Catherine Wheel
So many fireworks, but what's the big deal?

Everyone's staring up into the sky
Watching these silly explosions – but why?!
Watching this show and ignoring Jack Frost,
Well, I say, all fireworks, go away, get lost!

And this year I won't be left on the shelf,
Because I'll have the fireworks all to myself!
I'll steal Fizz's magic, and all will soon see,
That the star of the show is me, me, me!

The Magic Cupcake

Contents

Cross Your Fingers

"I am SO excited!" Rachel Walker said to her best friend, Kirsty Tate.

"Me, too!" Kirsty replied with a grin. Then she whispered quietly, "I wonder if we'll have any fairy adventures."

The girls were on their way to visit Kirsty's grandparents for Fireworks Night.

The two best friends always had fun on their trips together, but they also had a special secret — they were friends with the fairies! They had shared many magical adventures together since they had first met on Rainspell Island.

"You girls are going to have a great time," said Mrs Tate, from the front seat. "My parents are so looking forward to having you. And Sundown Village Fireworks Festival is the best in the world! There'll be a cupcake party, a parade and then a huge fireworks display on the night itself."

"I can't wait!" Rachel exclaimed.

Mr Tate looked at

them in the rear-view mirror. "I wish we could stay the whole week, but your grandparents will take good care of you."

"You'll be back for the fireworks, won't you?" Kirsty asked.

"We wouldn't miss it," Mr Tate promised.

The next thing they knew, everyone was piling out of the Tates' car and heading to the door of a beautiful cottage. There was a pathway with large stepping stones, and an ivy-covered arch over the doorway. The roof was even covered in grass!

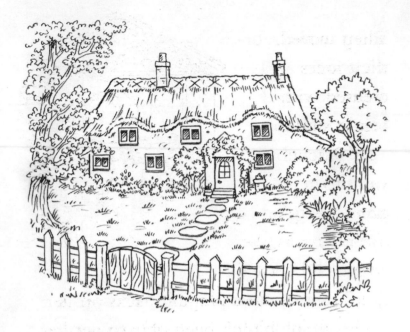

As Rachel closed her car door, she heard a strange noise – like a tiny, tiny firework.

"Did you hear that?" she asked Kirsty, looking around.

Kirsty shook her head.

"Well, hello!" Kirsty's grandparents called from the open door. "Welcome!"

They waved,
their faces
creased with
bright smiles.

As Rachel
went to
greet Kirsty's
grandparents, she
convinced herself
that her ears were playing tricks on her.
After all, she hadn't been able to get her
mind off fairies all morning.

Kirty's grandparents led everyone
inside. They had laid out a lunch of
turkey sandwiches and potato salad, with
chocolate cake for dessert.

After lunch, Rachel fiddled with
her napkin, distracted. She had heard
the same tiny explosions all through

lunch. She was having a hard time concentrating, and Kirsty's grandparents kept asking her lots of questions.

"We are thrilled to be sharing this special week with you, girls," Kirsty's grandfather said as he dished out some extra-tall pieces of triple-chocolate cake.

"None for me, thank you," Rachel said. "The lunch was delicious, and I'm completely full!"

Kirsty looked at her friend, concerned. Rachel had a faraway look in her eyes. Kirsty was confused.

It wasn't like Rachel to turn down dessert!

"Could we please be excused?" Kirsty asked, glancing from her grandparents to her parents. "We still need to bring in our suitcases, and I'd love to show Rachel where we'll be sleeping."

"No cake for you, either?" asked
Kirsty's grandfather, looking disappointed.
"It's our favourite family recipe."

"Maybe we could have some this
afternoon? It will taste especially good
after we get settled in," Kirsty said. She
absolutely loved chocolate cake, but she
had a feeling she and Rachel should
have a talk, in private.

"Of course, dear," Kirsty's grandmother
said with a smile.

"Thank you," Kirsty said, getting up
from her chair. She tapped Rachel on the
shoulder, and she stood up too. "We'll be
outside."

"Don't go too far," Mrs Tate called,
after they'd left the room. "Your dad and
I will have to head back before too long."

"We won't," Kirsty assured her mum,

but then Rachel grabbed her hand, tugged her through the door, and ran towards the garden at full speed.

BOOM! BOOM! BOOM!

"Rachel, what is it?" Kirsty asked, as the two girls raced across the lawn.

"I'm not sure," Rachel admitted, when they finally came to a stop. "But something told me we just had to get outside and into the garden." Rachel caught her breath. "I just couldn't sit there any more."

"I understand. I started to feel the same way," Kirsty said. "It was like I could hear tiny explosions in my head all through lunch. Is that what you were talking about when we first got here?"

"Do they start with a soft fizzing sound and then get louder?" Rachel asked.

Kirsty nodded.

"I think we're both hearing the same thing! I'm glad it's not just in my head!" Rachel said. "I think they're coming from over there." Rachel motioned to a large collection of garden gnomes, and the two friends hurried towards them.

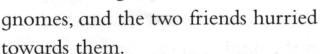

22

The tallest gnome had a lopsided grin and polka-dotted braces. As she looked, Kirsty noticed a faint stream of sparkles begin to shoot up from his pointy red hat.

Kirsty looked at her friend. Rachel gave her an encouraging smile. Kirsty reached out. Just as her hand brushed against the garden gnome, a series of tiny, sparkling fireworks erupted into the air.

BOOM! BOOM! BOOM!

As soon as the fireworks dissipated, a small fairy appeared, her glittery wings lifting her into the air. The wand she held was spouting rainbow sparkles that lit up like fireworks. The fairy looked sporty and fun in red leggings and a blue-  and-white striped shirt with a light blue cardigan. Her light brown skin practically glowed, and her wavy brown hair cascaded past her shoulders.

"Hooray! You're here!" the fairy cheered. "I was getting worried, waiting so long, but all my friends back in Fairyland said I could count on you. It's my pleasure to finally meet you, Kirsty and Rachel. My name is Fizz the Fireworks Fairy."

The girls took turns introducing themselves. Finally, Kirsty asked the question that was on both their minds. "Fizz, what are you doing here in Sundown? Is Jack Frost up to his old tricks again?"

The girls could hardly count the times they'd had to go up against him and his troublemaking goblins.

"I'm afraid so." Fizz nodded. "It all started when he complained about being tired and bored. One of his goblins suggested that he go and watch a firework show. Jack Frost really liked the idea." Fizz put her hands on her hips, and a scowl replaced the smile on her face. "Well, he did at first. But then, the goblins started getting too excited about fireworks, and Jack Frost felt left out. He decided that he didn't want *anyone* to enjoy any fireworks, if it meant he wouldn't be the centre of attention. And so he… Here, you can see for yourself. My magic bubble will replay the important scenes for us."

Fizz lifted her wand, and out of it
burst a pale blue firework that grew
to the size of a large puddle. When
the sparkles faded, a clear bubble was
in its place. Inside the bubble was a
picture of a cosy toadstool cottage with
a red, polka-dotted roof.

"That's my house," Fizz explained. "And those goblins were *not* invited."

Rachel and Kirsty gasped as they watched what happened next. The goblins snuck into the house and stole three items, one by one.

"Jack Frost sent his goblins after my three magical objects, because he wanted to have the magic of fireworks all to himself," Fizz said sadly. "As the Fireworks Fairy, it's my job to make sure everyone enjoys fireworks displays, both in the human world and in Fairyland! But without my magical objects, everything will start to go wrong. I know Jack Frost and his goblins are somewhere here in Sundown. Will you help me find them, before they ruin the fireworks festival for everyone?"

Rachel and Kirsty looked at each other and held hands. "Of course we will!" they said together.

The Missing Magic

"OK," Fizz began. "As you know, there isn't much time. This whole week is jam-packed with fun events in Sundown. As long as the goblins have my objects, anything could go wrong."

Kirsty and Rachel listened closely.

"First, we need to find my magic cupcake," Fizz explained. The girls must have looked puzzled, because Fizz hurried on:

"You know how you need to follow a recipe to make great cake?" The girls nodded. "Well, you also need to follow a plan for Fireworks Nights. Without the cupcake, no one will be able to plan things properly, and nothing will turn out the way people want it to."

"That makes sense," Kirsty said. "We'll try to find that first."

"What are the other magical objects?" Rachel asked. "Just so we'll be prepared."

"The second is a string of bunting," answered Fizz.

"Bunting? What's that?" Kirsty wondered aloud.

"You've seen bunting before," Fizz assured her. "It's all those strings of cute, colourful cloth triangles. Bunting is often used at the opening of a new shop, or at street parties."

"Oh, I love that stuff!" Kirsty responded.

"Me, too," said Fizz with a smile. "Especially this string. It helps make sure that everyone remembers their own traditions and favourite things about Fireworks Night. Without it, people will start to lose interest in the things they usually enjoy most."

"And the last object is my magic sparkler," Fizz said. "It is what gives

fireworks everywhere
their 'bang'. Unless we
find that sparkler, no
fireworks anywhere
are going to make
any noise or look at
all spectacular. You'll be
able to tell it's mine, though,
because it never goes out."

Both girls nodded, feeling relieved that
they had a plan for rescuing Fireworks
Night.

Just then, the door to the grass-roofed
cottage opened. Kirsty's grandparents
and parents came out. "I don't
understand why you would make the
cake without a recipe. That's just silly,"
Grandma said, in a playful but scolding
tone. "If it's an old family recipe, you

need to follow the recipe."

Grandpa didn't respond. He just shuffled around looking grumpy.

"Uh-oh," Fizz said. "It looks like the troubles are already starting."

"And it looks like my parents are leaving," Kirsty pointed out.

"Quick, Fizz, you can hide in my pocket," Rachel offered, tugging on the loose fabric of her dress so the fairy could slip in.

The girls hurried over and gave the Tates big hugs.

"I can't believe we won't see you until the weekend," Mrs Tate said, kissing Kirsty on the head.

"I'm sure you'll find a way to keep busy," Mr Tate added.

"I'm sure we will," Kirsty said with a

giggle, as she snuck a glance at the little lump in Rachel's pocket.

We All Scream for Ice Cream

Later that day, Kirsty's grandparents offered to take the two girls to the bake sale in the centre of town. They both jumped at the chance — not only would it be a treat, but it was the perfect place to look for Fizz's cupcake!

"We're almost there," Grandpa announced. "This path comes out right onto the high street.

The girls soon heard the voices of a gathering. Kirsty kept her eyes out for goblins, but she didn't see any.

"Here we are," Grandpa said.

Kirsty and Rachel marvelled at the bake sale. There were at least forty tables, each one with a different kind of cupcake or ice cream on it!

But something wasn't right. No one looked very happy. How could that be, with so many delicious treats all around?

"What do you mean, you forgot the sugar?" one woman asked another.

"I thought I knew the recipe by heart," the other answered. "I guess I didn't."

There seemed to be something wrong

with the treats at every table they passed. "This isn't what it's usually like,"

Grandpa noted. "It's usually crowded with happy people."

Rachel knew exactly what was happening. As long as the goblins had Fizz's magic cupcake, no one's plans were

working out. If this carried on, any plans
for Fireworks Night were sure to be a
disaster.

"We have to find that cupcake!" Kirsty
said.

Suddenly, they noticed a crowd at
the other end of the street. People were
jumping up and down with money in
their hands.

"I wonder why so many people are crowded around that table?" Kirsty murmured to Rachel.

"I'll find out," Fizz said, and darted over. A moment later, she fluttered back down and hid back in Rachel's hair. "You won't believe this," she began, "but it's two goblins. And it looks like they are selling my magic cupcake to the highest bidder!"

"W–what?" Kirsty stammered. "They can't do that! They'll ruin everything!"

Super Delicious

Over at the goblins' table, Kirsty and Rachel groaned. People had taken all the money they had out of their pockets and were waving it in the air.

"Ten pounds!" shouted one woman, excitedly.

"I'll double that!" called a man in a smart suit, rudely barging her out of the way.

The girls had just started to count their money, when Kirsty gasped. She realised it wouldn't be a good idea. It would be playing into the goblins' greedy hands!

"That cupcake has some seriously strong magic," she said to Rachel and Fizz. "It almost made us want to buy it!"

"We've got to get my cupcake before someone eats it!" Fizz warned. "Who knows what would happen then?"

The next thing they knew, Grandpa had shouldered his way over to the table. His thumbs were tugging on his braces, and he had a scowl on his face. "Now see here," he began. "Is there really only one cupcake? Because that is not fair at all."

The girls had inched close enough now to see the cupcake. It was beautiful. It seemed to glow. The frosting was thickly spread on top of the butter-coloured cake. Rachel's mouth began to water.

"He has a point," the suited man said, suddenly turning his gaze to the goblins. "Why is there only one cupcake? Where are the others from this batch?"

"Um," the goblin wearing a chef's hat began.

"Are you trying to swindle us?" the man asked, his voice gruff.

The goblins looked at each other, not seeming to know how to respond.

Kirsty crossed her fingers hopefully. Rachel could feel Fizz fidgeting on her shoulder, under her hair. "Just wait," she reassured the fairy. "I think we're about to get our chance."

"I don't trust you," Grandpa said to the goblins.

"Nor do I," said the other man.

Without a word, one of the goblins snatched up the cupcake. "Run," yelled the other. They took off down the street, dodging tables as they raced off.

"Cupcake imposters!" someone declared. "Let's go after them!"

Rachel, Kirsty and Grandpa followed the angry crowd after the goblins.

The goblins did their best to escape, but as they turned a sharp corner, they bumped into each other – and the cupcake went flying into the air.

But so did Fizz! The girls held their breath as she zoomed upwards. One second, the cupcake was whirling over their heads, and then it had vanished.

A glittering shower of fairy dust settled over the bake sale. The customers' anger was forgotten as it cleared to reveal the most beautiful array of cakes and sweet treats the girls had ever seen.

"That was fast!" Rachel said. The fairy must have already returned the precious cupcake to Fairyland and sent some special magic their way.

The two friends smiled at each other. They were one-third of the way to saving the Sundown Village Fireworks Festival!

The Brilliant
Bunting

Contents

No Sound Like Silence

"Still no sign of Fizz," Rachel said, looking out of the window. "Why haven't we heard anything?"

"I don't know," Kirsty answered, shaking her head.

It had been two days since they had rescued Fizz's magic cupcake, and the girls hadn't seen Fizz since. They both wondered where she could be.

"What should we do?" Rachel asked. The sky was very grey, and the clouds made her feel lazy.

"I'm not sure," Kirsty answered, putting on her flowery trainers. "But I bet there are more fun things happening today."

"One nice thing about staying with Grandma and Grandpa," Kirsty said, "is they always feed you like it's a big holiday."

Rachel felt her stomach rumble. "I love family traditions like that," she said. "I

56

wonder what's for breakfast!"

The girls hurried out of the guest bedroom and down the stairs to the dining room, but there wasn't anyone there. All they found was a note.

Grab some cereal and a banana.
Milk is in the fridge (obviously).
See you later,
Grandma

"How odd," Kirsty said, feeling a bit sad. "They didn't even say goodbye," she mumbled.

"Are you thinking what I'm thinking?" Rachel asked.

"This has to be because the goblins have Fizz's other two magic objects?" Kirsty said.

"Yes," Rachel replied. "Definitely. Let's take those bananas and get to work. The Sundown Village Fireworks Festival is this weekend, so there's no time to lose."

As they left the cosy, grassed-topped cottage, the girls went over what they knew about the situation with the goblins and Jack Frost.

"There were three missing objects. We found the first one, the magic cupcake, in the bakery in town," Rachel said.

"So there are still two magic objects missing," Kirsty added. "One is the bunting, the decoration with all the colourful triangles hanging from it. The other is a sparkler that doesn't go out."

"Exactly," Rachel agreed. "So we are looking for those two things, and they could be anywhere."

Kirsty nodded. "The goblins actually had the cupcake, so maybe they have the other things too."

The girls made their way along the pavement. "It's so quiet," Rachel  commented. "Where is everyone?"

"Maybe they're all in town," Kirsty suggested. "Because it's coming up to Fireworks Night, there are lots of things going on." But when the pavement came to the high street, the girls still didn't see many people around. When they passed the playground, it was empty.

"Let's check the town calendar," Kirsty

suggested, pointing to what looked like a large outdoor bulletin board. It had a wooden frame with lots of papers tacked to it.

"There's a parade this afternoon," Kirsty said.

"But not much right now," Rachel said, looking around at the quiet street and not knowing what to do. "You know

what Queen Titania would say?"

Kirsty nodded. "Let the magic come to you." It was the Queen of Fairyland's reminder that fairy magic would help them out when the time was right.

"Maybe we should get a morning muffin and wait," Rachel suggested.

The girls headed to the bakery, but when they got there, it was closed! A man in a baker's hat had just locked the door. "Not enough business," he grumbled. "Everyone's eating ice cream instead!" The man shook his fist at a shop down the street.

"That's weird," Kirsty said, striding in that direction. "It's a bit cold for ice cream."

"Even more weird, look at that line," Rachel said. "Where did all these people come from?" As they turned the corner onto another street, the girls saw a line that went out of the shop and several doors down. "And why do they want ice cream at 10 o' clock in the morning?"

Pssst. Pssst.

"Did you hear that?"

Pssst. Pssst.

"Look! In that tree," Kirsty said. "It's Fizz!"

"Finally!" Rachel said, with a happy grin, and the two girls rushed over to greet their newest fairy friend.

Breakfast Ice Cream

"Everything's muddled up," Fizz whispered. "No one is enjoying their usual traditions."

"I think ice cream for breakfast could be a good, new tradition for me," Rachel said, rubbing her stomach.

"It sounds good," Fizz agreed, "but look at the people coming out."

The girls turned and watched as several
small groups exited the ice-cream parlour.
Everyone was carrying a single scoop
of vanilla on a wafer cone, and no one
appeared to be happy.

"That's odd," Kirsty said. "This is one
of those fancy ice-cream shops where

they use homemade brownies and cookie dough and all kinds of other stuff to make exciting flavours. So why is everyone ordering vanilla?"

"That's a good question," Rachel said. "Especially if it doesn't make them happy."

"Oh, look! There's Grandpa," Kirsty said, pointing to him. He was next in line to order. "Vanilla is actually his favourite, so he will be glad when he comes out." The girls and Fizz watched closely.

But the clerk with the scoop shook his head at Grandpa. Grandpa immediately left the little shop with a scowl on his face. Fizz hid in Rachel's pocket as Kirsty waved to her grandpa. "Hey, Grandpa! Over here!"

Grandpa skulked his way over to the

girls. "Just my luck," he complained. "They ran out of vanilla just as soon as it was my turn."

"I'm sorry, Grandpa," Kirsty said. "That's disappointing. But can I ask what made you come to town for ice cream in the morning?"

"I don't know," he answered, with a shrug. "Grandma didn't feel like making breakfast, so we were going to go to the bakery. But then that seemed boring. We do it too much. I guess I'll just go home."

Kirsty and Rachel exchanged glances. Grandma and Grandpa were tired of

their own,
favourite
traditions!
This was not
good at all!

"I think it's
a sure sign
we need to

find my magic objects," Fizz declared.
"Any sign of the goblins?"

"No, none," Rachel replied. "But I see a
whole bag of bunting!"

"They're putting up all the town
decorations!" Kirsty said. "I wonder if the
magic bunting is in the bag?"

"Maybe! You'll know it because it
will be extra bright, and it will have a
magic glow," Fizz explained, with a spin.
She flew a loop and landed in Rachel's

pocket again, so the girls could approach the workers. "Can we help?" they asked.

Volunteering would be the easiest way to get a good look at the various strands of bunting.

Using a ladder, they helped string the colourful decorations from one side of the high street to the other.

"It looks like the sweetest town ever!" Rachel exclaimed.

"I wish there were some people around to see it," Kirsty said. It was like everyone who had come out for ice cream had gone home, grumpy.

"Well, I wish one of those strings of

bunting was magic, but none of them are," Fizz said, folding her arms while her wings flapped behind her. "How are we going to find it?

Roll Up, Roll Up!

"What's this?" Rachel asked, as they walked back down the high street and spotted a long rope.

"That's for the tug-of-war later," Kirsty replied. "They do it every year before Fireworks Night. Everyone usually comes out to watch."

"I'm not sure there will be much of a turnout today," Rachel said, looking around at the empty street.

"We need a whole crew of children to take part," said Kirsty. "Then the goblins are more likely to come out to join the fun, and we can see if they have the objects. Fizz, isn't there something you can do?"

"My wand just isn't very strong when my magic objects aren't in Fairyland," the fairy explained. "I can use it on one person, or on very small groups. But I can't get all the children to come out at once. I'm really sorry."

"Don't worry, Fizz," Kirsty reassured
the sad fairy. "I have an idea. Could you
magic up a megaphone?"

"That I can do," said Fizz, with a smile.
In a flash of fairy sparkles, Kirsty found
herself holding a bright red megaphone.

She marched over
to a row of houses.
"Roll up, roll up!
Time for the tug-of-
war!" she yelled into the
megaphone.

A door opened in one of
the houses. "Yes?" A little girl
with a yellow T-shirt and
blue trousers appeared, with
her father behind her.

"Hi!" Rachel greeted her. "My name's

Rachel. My friend Kirsty and I want
to do the tug-of-war. Will you play
with us?"

Just as Rachel asked the question,
Fizz sent a single stream of sparkles that

swirled all around the
girl. The girl smiled.
"I'd love to," she
said.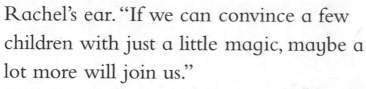

"That's perfect,"
Fizz whispered in
Rachel's ear. "If we can convince a few
children with just a little magic, maybe a
lot more will join us."

Every child they saw looked really
bored, but Fizz's magic perked them right
up. Soon, children started to show up on
their own. After a little while, they had
two full teams, ready to compete!

Rachel and Kirsty were ready, too. Fizz
was now hidden in a pocket of Rachel's
T-shirt. "Keep an eye out for goblins," the
fairy whispered.

Luckily, the girls ended up on the same

team. They took positions at one end of
the rope.

"The other team is all boys," a girl with
plaits said. "We'll show them."

"I don't think I know any of them,"
said a boy. "It's hard to tell, with those
big caps on their heads."

Big caps? Kirsty and Rachel had seen

that before! "Goblins!" they whispered to each other.

"Ready, set, tug!" someone yelled.

Kirsty held tight. Rachel was right in front of her. "Can you see them?" Kirsty grunted.

"No," Rachel said, through gritted teeth. "We'll have to wait. These goblins aren't that big, but they're strong."

The whole team stumbled forward, and the front two children fell across the line.

"We won! We won!" the other team all chanted together. "We are the winners, and you are the losers. We won!"

"They are not very nice winners," Kirsty said, scowling. Now that she could see the other team, it was clear that they were goblins.

Fizz peeked out of Rachel's pocket.

"Can you see one of my magic objects?" she asked hopefully.

Both girls craned their necks to get better views.

"No," they both answered, shaking their heads.

Kirsty looked frustrated. "What if they hid them somewhere and aren't going to bring them out?" she worried out loud. "The big firework display is tomorrow night. We have to find both objects before then, or it could be a disaster."

"That's a good point," Fizz said, scratching her chin with one finger. "But let's give this a try. If one of the objects is close, its magic will help the goblins enjoy all the fun traditions even more. I don't think they'll be able to resist taking part in all the festivities."

"You're right," Rachel agreed. "We'll just have to watch them very closely."

"We won't let them out of our sight," promised Kirsty, and she took her friend by the hand.

True Teamwork

Kirsty gave Rachel's hand a tug and the two rushed over to the other team. "Hi!" Kirsty said to the goblins. "We'd love to be on your team this time around. You are really good."

"Oh," a goblin wearing thick gloves said. "Well, thank you. We just love tug of war."

"Yes, so much fun!" said another goblin, who was wearing sunglasses. "Please join us. You can be at the end."

"They're being so nice," Rachel said under her breath to Kirsty.

"Yes," whispered Fizz. "They are very enthusiastic. They love the game so much, I suspect that my bunting might be close by. It helps people cherish old traditions even more."

"OK then," Kirsty said, in a hushed voice. "We'll be on the lookout, and

we won't give ourselves
away."

"Great!" Fizz said.

All three friends
felt good to have a
plan, but it wasn't
easy pretending they
didn't know who
the goblins were.

"Are you ready?" the
first goblin asked. "It's a shame you don't
have gloves. With gloves, the rough rope
doesn't hurt your hands."

"They really want to win," Kirsty said
to Rachel and Fizz in a low tone.

"That's another sign that they have the
bunting," Fizz said. "They are really well
prepared. The magic bunting helps with
that."

From where she was standing, Rachel could see almost all the goblins. There were some who were doing the tug-of-war; others were just cheering on from the sidelines. But no one was holding the colourful decoration with cloth triangles. "No sign of the bunting yet," Rachel said.

"Ready, set, tug!"

Rachel and Kirsty gripped the rope. They pulled back. Without trying very hard, they found they could take a step back. "We're pulling the other team over," Rachel said.

"Yes, we're winning!" Kirsty said excitedly.

"Heave!" the goblins chanted in chorus. "Ho!" Each time they called out, they gave a giant tug. "Heave!" they

chanted again. "Ho!"

It seemed that they were just seconds from getting the other team across the line – and winning – when Kirsty tripped on a large root. She lost her balance and fell to the ground. Rachel tumbled on top of her. Then the goblin right in front of Rachel stumbled backward. "Yikes!" he yelled. "Grab the rope!"

But it was too late. All the goblins began to drop, one by one. And each one dropped the rope as he fell. Soon, the goblin with the thick gloves was the last one standing. He didn't realise that the rest of his team was out of the game.

"Heave!" he yelled alone, but no one else pulled. It was the other team that managed to make a mighty yank. They dragged the lone goblin over the line.

Their team
members
gathered in a
tight huddle
to celebrate.

The goblins
all scowled.

"You!" a goblin snarled, pointing at
Kirsty and Rachel. "It's your fault we
didn't win!"

The girls were still on the ground.

"I'm really sorry," Kirsty
replied. "I tripped."

"It's more fun
when we win,"
the goblin pouted.

"It'll be OK,"
the first goblin
said. "There are

other fun things to do today. It's almost time for the parade! Hurry up – get an outfit from home, or borrow one from the Sundown collection!"

A quiet hum began to grow. Soon, almost everyone who had come out for the tug-of-war was busy talking about their fun plans for the parade. They began to head home to get ready.

"Keep on eye on that goblin," Fizz said.

"I will," replied Rachel. "He's great! He just got everyone excited for the parade, including me!"

"Yes," answered Fizz. "That's why
I think he has my bunting. Just you
watch."

All Dressed Up

"Let's look for costumes at the fancy dress shop," said Kirsty.

"Good idea," said Rachel.

But when they arrived at the shop, it was in a terrible mess.

"This is a disaster!" Rachel groaned, picking up a boa that didn't have many feathers left.

"Goblins," Kirsty whispered, examining a group of children nearby wearing strange costumes. When the girls looked closely, they could see the goblins' green skin under their make-up.

The girls looked through the remaining costumes. "There isn't much left," Rachel noted. "We'll have to piece something together." They draped cloth over their shoulders, and looped belts around their waists to form togas.

"We're Greek goddesses!" Kirsty smiled.

"You look great!" Fizz said. "Now, let's track down that enthusiastic goblin. We have to figure out if he has my bunting, and how to get it back."

The girls went hand in hand through the crowd.

"When is the parade supposed to start?" Rachel asked.

"In less than an hour," Kirsty said.

"Then we don't have much time," Rachel said.

"Don't worry," Fizz whispered, from her hiding place in Rachel's pocket. "Let the magic come to you."

Just as Fizz said it, the girls spotted someone dancing on the edge of the crowd, all by himself. He seemed to be waltzing. Holding one arm up and another in front of him, he took elegant sweeping steps and made graceful spins.

"That's our goblin!" Kirsty exclaimed, in a hushed voice.

"Yes! It is," agreed Fizz. "Check out his beautiful skirt."

When the girls looked closer, they realised that his full, many-coloured skirt was the bunting! He had wrapped it around and around his waist to make a very stylish skirt that glittered with magic.

"How much magic do you have left in your wand?" Rachel asked Fizz.

"Just a little," Fizz admitted.

"Do you have enough to make a real costume?" Rachel asked.

Kirsty immediately understood what Rachel was thinking. "Yes!" she said. "A costume that would fit in at a real ball. A true gown!"

Rachel smiled and nodded.

"Well, we can find out!" Fizz gave her wand a mighty swirl, and sparkles came out with a *whoosh*! All at once, the most gorgeous gown appeared, floating in mid-air! It was an elegant midnight blue satin, with lace and ruffles on the sleeves and a full skirt that reached the ground. It also had a wig with hair looped in a tall bun.

"Nice work!" Rachel exclaimed. "Now we just have to get the goblin to swap."

The girls took the costume and approached the dancing goblin.

"Excuse me," Rachel began. "I am sorry to interrupt, but I couldn't help but notice your lovely dancing."

The goblin halted at once, his eyes filled with delight. "Really?" he asked.

"Yes," Kirsty responded. "Are you here for the parade?"

"Why, yes," the goblin said. "I love the chance to dress up. What a grand tradition."

"Well," said Rachel. "We were wondering if you would like to try on this special costume. It looks like it would be just your size."

The goblin reached out and touched the satin fabric. "Ooh!" he squealed in delight. He scrambled out of his old outfit and put on the dress. Then he snatched the wig from Rachel's hands.

Meanwhile, Fizz had burst out of Kirsty's pocket and swept towards the bunting. As soon as she touched it, it shrank back down to Fairyland size. In an instant, both Fizz and the bunting were gone.

Suddenly, the high street was full of people in costume. The parade was beginning!

"Wow!" Kirsty said. "Fizz must have done some speedy work again. Everything came together so fast!"

"That bunting must have powerful magic," Rachel said. Then, in the blink of an eye, the girls were no longer wearing their simple Greek goddess costumes. Kirsty was dressed as a pirate, complete with beard, and a parrot on her shoulder. Rachel, wearing golden armour and carrying a bow and arrow, was an elf warrior.

"These are by far the coolest costumes ever!" Kirsty said.

"And this will be the coolest parade," Rachel added, "because it is such a cool town tradition."

With that, the two girls took their places with all the people, goblins, pets, horse carriages, clowns, jugglers and stilt walkers. Kirsty and Rachel were happy to enjoy the fun for now. But tomorrow, they would have a magic sparkler to find!

The Sizzling Sparkler

Contents

Tiresome Troubles

Both Kirsty and Rachel woke up early.
Fizz was flying around their room
in excitement. It was the day of the
Sundown Village Fireworks Festival!

"We must find the magic sparkler
today," said Rachel, brushing her
hair. "Otherwise the display is going
to be a big disaster."

Just then, they heard a knock at the front door. "I'll get it," Kirsty offered.

When she came back to the bedroom, she told Rachel that it had been some children from the tug-of-war game the day before. "They want us to be part of their team. Today is the Sundown Challenge. It's a mix of obstacle courses and other games."

"It sounds like fun," Rachel said.

"But what about the magic sparkler?" Kirsty asked. "How will we search for it if we are also taking part in the challenge?"

"Remember Queen Titania's advice," said Fizz. "You should let the magic come to you."

After the girls ate some of Grandma's delicious eggy bread, they headed out to the town centre. Small groups of children were already gathering.

"Hey! Over here!" one of them called. "You're just in time. We're doing an obstacle course first. Then there's a treasure hunt. And tonight, right before the fireworks, there will be a huge game of hide-and-seek. We play it every year."

"That sounds like a great plan," Rachel said, feeling excited.

A grown-up was holding a megaphone very similar to the one Fizz had magicked up the day before. He got the groups in order, then announced the stages of the race. "First, you run through the tyres," he began, "then you go over the hay-bale pyramid. Finally, you climb the giant cargo net and then slide down one of the ropes on the other side."

"This looks like fun!" Kirsty said.

"Ready, set, go!" the man with the megaphone shouted.

The first boy ran straight for the tyre obstacle. When he stepped in the middle of the first tyre, there was a huge, muddy splash. It went up to the very top of his football sock! The girl next to him slipped in the muck and landed with a thud. Only the boy on the far end escaped without being slowed down by the dirty puddles.

"Maybe it's because of his big feet," Kirsty thought out loud.

Rachel turned to her friend and
gripped her hand.
"Goblins!" they
exclaimed
together.

"That's no
good," Rachel
said. "They're
going to cause
all kinds of
trouble for the
other teams
in the challenge."

"But what really matters is that they're
here," Rachel reminded her friend. "If
they're doing the Sundown Challenge, we
have a better chance of keeping track of
them. Maybe we'll even spot Fizz's final
missing object."

"You're right! I have a good feeling about this. We'll find that magic sparkler and give it back to Fizz," Kirsty declared. "I'm sure of it."

Even More Obstacles

Unfortunately, the goblins – and their big feet – were really far ahead. They were very fast on the obstacle course.

Now it was Rachel's turn. She splashed through the tyres, getting very wet and messy – but didn't slow down. Then

she came to the hay-bale pyramid. She
climbed carefully, and was almost at the
top when she felt something pull her
foot. She gave it a yank, but she couldn't
move. Then, all at once, she started to
sink through the
hay. Her
whole body
scraped
through
the prickly
edges, and
she landed

with a thud on the
ground. She was *inside* the pyramid, and
it was dark.

"Hello?" she said in a small voice, but
no one answered. "Who's there?" Rachel
pushed herself to her feet. She felt very

alone, although she had a bad feeling that she was not.

Suddenly, she heard a different sound. It was a rustling. She looked up and saw a bright sliver of sky overhead. It was the crack where she had fallen through the hay.

"Rachel?" a voice called. Then a face peeked in, covering the crack. It was Kirsty!

Kirsty eased through the gap and landed on her feet.

"What are you doing here?" Rachel asked. "We can't have two people on the course at the same time. It's a relay."

"But the relay isn't really that important," Kirsty said. "Remember?"

Of course Kirsty was right. Rachel knew that.

"I thought I should help you get out of here," Kirsty said. "I didn't think it would be so dark. Don't worry – one of the others is coming with a rope."

Hmm, hmm.

"What was that?" Kirsty asked.

Hmm, hmm, the sound came again, followed by a deep breath. "It's me," someone said. "From the parade. The one with the great dress and the wig."

"Oh!" Rachel said, remembering the goblin that Fizz had helped.

"What are you doing in here?" Kirsty asked.

"They told me to hide in here and pull you down once you reached the top," said the goblin's voice, sounding sheepish. "But now I know it's you, I wish I hadn't."

"That's awful!" Rachel insisted. "That's cheating!"

"I'm sorry," the goblin said. "But I can help."

"Help?" Rachel felt her heart flutter with hope. Would he tell them where the magic sparkler was?

"You don't need a rope to get out," he said. "There's a secret door."

Rachel sighed. He wasn't going to tell them where the third magic object was, but escaping the hay pyramid was a start at least.

"Watch," the goblin said. The girls heard the sound of something being scooted across the ground. In just a moment, a block of light appeared. The goblin kneeled down and stuck his head in the hole.

"I really loved that costume yesterday," he said. "It was so nice of

you to share it." When he crawled back out, the girls could see there was a smile on his face. "It's all clear," he whispered. "You should go now. Quick!"

Scavengers!

The girls quickly thanked the goblin, and sneaked back to their team.

"How did you get here?" one of the children whispered when he saw them. "Everyone thinks you're still in the pyramid."

The girls explained that they had found an exit. They did not explain that a goblin had showed it to them!

"Don't worry about not finishing the course," another boy said. "It's time for the scavenger hunt! Here is our first clue."

WHERE DOES THE BREAD RISE BEFORE YOU DO?

"That's a weird clue," the boy said. "How do they know when I get up?"

"Maybe this is a place that opens up really early, every day," Rachel suggested.

"And a place that makes bread," Kirsty hinted.

"The bakery!" the whole team chanted together, and headed off down the high street.

The baker looked up as they walked in. "Hello! What can I get for you?"

"We were wondering if you might have a clue for the treasure hunt," Kirsty said.

"I do," the baker said, with a smile. "For you I have a clue, and muffins, too."

The team left the shop clutching blueberry oat muffins. Kirsty held out the clue, so everyone could read.

WHERE DOES THE TIME GO? IN SUNDOWN, IT WINDS UP AND WINDS DOWN HERE.

"That's got to be at the old clocktower in town," Kirsty said. "It's just down the road."

When they arrived, they looked all around the old building and the tower. They ran to the back of the building and found

a door. It was old and red, and creaked
when it opened. They ran up the steps
and saw big, turning gears, and a large
sign.

THE SPARKS START HERE!
AT LEAST, THEY DID ONCE UPON
A TIME.

"Oh! It sounds like a fairy tale," a girl
said.

"I don't think it's a fairy tale," said
Rachel. "I think it's more like history."

"I know!" said Kirsty. "It must be
the Fireworks Museum. It used to be a
factory, where fireworks were made."

But at that moment, they heard cackles
and the scurry of big feet.

"Goblins!" Rachel whispered to Kirsty.

"Maybe they have the magic sparkler with them!"

"We have to get it," Rachel said, with a determined look on her face. She turned to the others. "Come on — we've got to get to that museum!"

The team stopped at a high, iron gate and took a long look at the Fireworks Museum.

"The fireworks they made here were famous," Kirsty said. "Half the town of Sundown worked here a long time ago."

"Are you part of the treasure hunt?" a man in the ticket booth asked. He had a long white mustache and tiny round glasses.

"Yes, we are," Kirsty said.

"Then you get in for free," he said.

"Thank you," the group said together.

"Well, you're welcome," he answered, handing them a map. "You're much more polite than that other group. They just ran straight in without saying anything."

Kirsty and Rachel exchanged a glance.

"Good luck!" said the man.

The team headed through the gate and entered the brass doors of the museum, looking for the next clue.

At that moment, Rachel saw something flash in the corner of her eye. 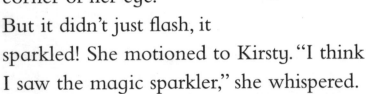 But it didn't just flash, it sparkled! She motioned to Kirsty. "I think I saw the magic sparkler," she whispered.

"Maybe we should split up," Kirsty suggested to the rest of the group. "We'll go that way."

The two best friends hurried off down a long corridor. They knew that there were some things that they needed to do on their own.

Fake Firecracker

Rachel and Kirsty ran down the long hallway. The museum had lots of narrow tables with old papers and tall piles of colourful tubes.

"Are those old fireworks?" Rachel wondered out loud.

"I think so," Kirsty replied.

"I'm not sure this is safe," said Rachel. "If what I saw *was* the sparkler, it would be very dangerous to light it in here. It's full of fireworks."

"You're right," Kirsty said. "But it's Fizz's *magic* sparkler. I'm sure it's safe."

"I wish that were true," said a voice behind them. It was Fizz!

"Fizz!" Rachel said. "We think your sparkler is here somewhere!"

"Me, too," said the little fairy. "Unfortunately, it isn't acting like it should."

"What do you mean?" Kirsty asked.

"Well," Fizz began to explain, "my sparkler is magical. It *is* very safe, as long as I am the one who is holding it. But when someone else has it, it could be dangerous. We must find it as soon as we can!"

The two girls and one fairy peeked around a corner. Right next to a wall of old, empty gunpowder barrels, the goblins were arguing. It looked like each goblin wanted a turn with the sparkler. They were all grabbing at it, but the goblin who had it kept yanking it away.

"This might not be that easy," Fizz admitted.

"They got along much better when they were focused on winning the Sundown Challenge," Kirsty commented.

"Yes, they worked together much better then," added Rachel.

At that moment, they heard their names. The other children were calling for them.

"Oh, no!" Kirsty said. "The goblins will hear!"

"Wait," Fizz said. "Maybe your teammates will help

distract the goblins."

"Kirsty! Rachel!" the calls were getting louder. "We found the next clue!"

The two girls raced down the stairs to meet their teammates. They heard the tiny flutter of fairy wings behind them. "The goblins heard everything!" Fizz declared. "They're already sneaking up behind us. This might be the fastest way to get them out of here."

Rachel sneaked glances over her shoulder as they ran. She wanted to make sure the greedy goblins were behind them. Luckily, the one with the sparkler was in front.

After they had left the museum and were back outside, the teammates stopped to catch their breath.

"What's the next clue?" Kirsty asked.

FLOWERS WILL EXPLODE AND THE SKY WILL QUAKE. MEET EVERYONE DOWN BY THE LAKE.

"They're talking about fireworks!" said Rachel. "We should head to the lake!"

They took the path that led to a clearing by the still lake. Kirsty and Rachel could hear the scampering of

footsteps behind them. The goblins
were right on their tail...but they
made it made it out before them. They
had won the treasure hunt! That meant
they were tied with the goblins.

"If we can win hide-and-seek, we'll end in first place," said one of the boys.

The last phase of the challenge was starting. The girls hurried off to find hiding places. No one knew that they were seeking goblins, too!

Dusk was falling quickly by now.

"This is kind of spooky," Rachel said, looking into the gathering dark.

"I agree," Kirsty said. "But it's also kind of fun."

Suddenly, Kirsty heard a big splash. The two friends hurried to the edge of the lake. In the dim light, they could see several figures on the old swimming dock. They were all leaning forward with their hands on their hips. Their long noses nearly touched as they argued.

Rachel counted four goblins . . . and one sparkler.

Boom, Bang, Sizzle, Cheer!

"How did they get out there?" Kirsty queried. The swimming dock was way out in the lake. She did not think goblins were very good swimmers.

"Look! They took canoes," Rachel
pointed out. There were two canoes
floating near the dock. "But *why* are
they out there? Isn't that where they are
setting off the fireworks later? And aren't
all the fireworks already on the dock?"

Kirsty looked closer and realised her
friend was right. There were several
bundles and some
crates by the goblins.
It looked like a lot
of equipment.

"Oh, no. Oh, no,
oh, no, oh, no," Fizz
mumbled as she flew
out of Rachel's pocket.
"This isn't good. If they
aren't careful, they could set off
every last firework. That would be

very dangerous!"

"And very sad," Kirsty added. "They really will ruin the Fireworks Night for everyone." Kirsty thought about her parents. They were so excited to sit down and enjoy the fireworks as a family, but they weren't even here yet. Neither were Grandpa and Grandma. It was one of their favourite Sundown traditions.

"We *have* to get my sparkler back," Fizz said.

"I have an idea," Rachel said. "It's a bit silly, but it just might work. Fizz, can you turn us both into fairies?"

With just a twirl of Fizz's wand, swirls of glitter whooshed around the girls and they felt themselves shrinking. Plus, they grew beautiful, shiny wings. Now, those wings carried them over the lake, so they

could get as
close to the
goblins as
possible –
without
being seen,
of course.

The three fairies
landed in a canoe. From there, they could
see the four goblins. The sparkler lit their
angry green faces. Not one of them was
happy. They all wanted the sparkler!

"So, are you ready to give it a try?"
Rachel asked.

"Absolutely," Fizz answered. Kirsty gave
a nod.

On the count of three, the three fairies
began to make their spookiest, most
haunting ghost sounds ever. *Wooooooo,*

woooooOOOO, wOOOOOOOOOOoooo.

The four goblins stopped bickering and began shaking in their shoes.

Next, Fizz pointed her wand at Kirsty. When Kirsty began to speak, sparkles spun in a tunnel around her mouth. Kirsty's voice came out as a deep groan, almost like a monster. It even frightened Rachel!

"I'm the ghost of the fireworks factory. You must give back the magic sparkler now!" Kirsty said. "I will haunt whoever has stolen the sparkler!"

At once, the goblin with the wand tried to give it to the goblin next to him. That goblin took it, but then passed it to the one next to him. "Not me, not me!" that goblin screamed, and he threw the sparkler up into the evening sky.

Quick as lightning, Fizz was in the air. She darted straight up and grasped her final magical object. As soon as it was in her hands, the sparkler shot out an enormous, beautiful burst of rainbow colour, raining down on everything in sight.

"Wahoo!" Fizz yelped with joy, as the sparkler turned back to fairy size.

"I'll make this the most spectacular fireworks show Sundown Village has ever seen!"

As she whirled in the sky, happy blasts of fireworks poured from her wand, landing on the equipment set up on the dock. As the magic sparkles faded, the equipment glowed with magic.

Kirsty and Rachel blinked to find that Fizz's blast of magic had sent them back to the edge of the lake and turned them back into humans. From there, they could see that the goblins had all jumped off

151

the dock and were swimming to shore.
Fizz was nowhere to be seen. Rachel and
Kirsty were certain she had returned to
Fairyland, so the magic sparkler was safe
and sound.

When the two friends walked out of
the woods, everything seemed very quiet.
"There they are!" a voice cried. "Finally!"

Their teammates were racing towards
them. "Where were you?" they asked.
"We looked everywhere!"

"I told them you probably hid in the
lake," one of the girls exlaimed.

"Not exactly," Kirsty replied.

"So, we won?" Rachel asked.

"Yes!" they all shouted in glee.

"But we don't get anything," a small
girl said, looking a bit sad. "There's no
prize for winning."

That's when Rachel felt something tingle in her sweater pocket. She reached in and pulled out a golden charm. It hung from a long chain and was in the shape of a sparkler. In the moonlight, it really seemed to glitter. Rachel was certain Fizz had put it there.

"Here," Rachel said. "You can have this." Kirsty smiled at her.

153

The little girl's
eyes grew wide.
"Really?" she
asked. She
reached out
and took the
charm in her
hand.

"Really," Kirsty said. "It was fun being
teammates with you."

The teammates all shared a hug, and
then everyone went to find their families
for the big fireworks show.

"Mum, Dad!" Kirsty cried when she
saw her parents. They were carrying
blankets and beach chairs. Grandma had
a full bag of snacks.

"I'm so happy to see you," Mrs Tate
said, giving her a big hug.

"I'm almost as excited to see you as I am to see these fireworks," Mr Tate added. "And that's saying something."

Everyone laughed, especially Kirsty. She was so relieved that Fizz had all her magical objects again.

"Thanks so much for having me," Rachel said to the Tate family. "I love Sundown. We've had a great time."

Kirsty smiled. "Thanks for coming, Rachel," she said. "It wouldn't have been the same without you."

The friends knew it was true. They were a real team when it came to helping the fairies.

Kirsty sat down and patted the blanket, so Rachel would sit, too.

"I have a feeling these will be the best fireworks yet," Mr Tate said.

"What makes you think that?" Grandpa asked.

"I'm not sure," Kirsty's dad answered. "I can't explain it. There's just something magical in the air."

Rachel and Kirsty smiled. The two best friends certainly agreed with that.

The End

Now it's time for Kirsty and
Rachel to help...

Elsa the Mistletoe Fairy

Read on for a sneak peek...

"Wheeeeee!"

Kirsty Tate and Rachel Walker zoomed
down the snowy hill on a sledge, cosily
wrapped up in their warmest clothes. All
they could hear was the swish-swoosh
of the sledge on the crisp snow. They
squealed with laughter as the sledge
plunged into a snowdrift at the bottom
of the hill, and they tumbled into the soft
whiteness.

Giggling and rosy-cheeked, the best
friends helped each other up and brushed
the snow from their winter coats. Their
breath puffed into the air like smoke.

Ahead of them, the roofs of Wetherbury village were heavy with snow.

"We have to leave the sledge here for the next person to pull back up the hill," said Kirsty. "While the roads are all covered in snow, it's the quickest way around the village."

"It's so quiet and beautiful," said Rachel. "I like it this way."

"Me too," Kirsty agreed. "This is going to be one of the most Christmassy Christmases ever."

Instead of cars roaring along the streets, children were out building snowmen in the middle of the road. Grown-ups and children were whizzing down the hills on shared sledges instead of walking, and everyone was taking their turn to pull the sledges back to the tops of the hills.

"I'm so happy you're staying with us

while the Wetherbury Christmas Market is running," Kirsty said as they scrunched their way towards the village centre. "It's on for three days — today, Saturday and Sunday — and it's so magical."

"Then I'm sure I'm going to love it," said Rachel, with a smile. "Magic seems to follow us around, doesn't it?"

Kirsty smiled too. Together, they had shared many secret adventures with their fairy friends, and they knew the tingling excitement of magic in the air. Just then, thick flakes of snow began to fall again, and the girls tucked their scarves around them even more tightly.

"If the snow keeps falling at this rate I won't just be here for three days," said Rachel. "I might be spending the whole of Christmas in Wetherbury!"

Kirsty looked up at the falling

snowflakes and grinned.

"Keep falling!" she shouted, throwing out her arms and twirling around. "I want my best friend to stay with me for ever!"

When they arrived in the middle of the village, it was already bustling with people. A red banner was hanging above the main street, covered with golden writing.

Welcome to Wetherbury Christmas Market!

Friday: Christmas decorations for home and tree

Saturday: Christmas food

Sunday: Christmas presents, cards and wrapping paper

Merry Christmas, everyone!

Below the banner, little stalls lined the street, sparkling with tinsel, coloured glass and sequinned decorations. The air was filled with the scents of cinnamon, roasted chestnuts and steaming hot chocolate. Rachel and Kirsty strolled from stall to stall, picking up delicate hand-painted glass baubles, thick garlands of tinsel and shiny holly wreaths.

"Everything looks and smells so good," said Rachel, pausing beside the roasted-chestnut stall. "Shall we share a bag of these?"

A few minutes later the girls were standing beside the mistletoe stall, their mittened hands around a warm paper bag full of chestnuts.

"These are delicious," said Kirsty, before popping another chestnut into her mouth. "I wish it could be Christmas all year round!"

They had slipped down the side of the mistletoe stall, sheltering from the flurries of snow in the narrow space between stalls. Kirsty glanced up and saw a few sprigs of mistletoe hanging down above them.

"The berries are almost as white as snow," she said. "Oh my goodness – one of them is glowing!"

Rachel and Kirsty gazed up at the single, shining mistletoe berry, and then looked at each other.

"Magic!" they said together.

The people walking along the street were browsing the stalls or keeping their heads down against the snow. None of them was looking down the narrow gap where the girls were standing. Rachel and Kirsty looked up again. The bright berry was swelling, just like a balloon being blown up. It grew bigger and bigger until . . . POP! It burst with a jingling of tiny bells, and a little fairy was fluttering it its place.

"Hello!" said the fairy in a bright voice. "I'm Elsa the Mistletoe Fairy."

Her dress was the colour of a mistletoe berry, and her shoes glittered like snow in the sunshine. She shook back her golden hair and smiled at the girls.

"It's lovely to meet you," said Rachel. "You must be one of the fairies that looks after Christmas?"

Elsa nodded. "It's my job to make sure that every Christmas is better than the one before," she said. "We want everyone's year to end happily – especially yours! I've come to invite you both to King Oberon and Queen

Titania's Royal Christmas Gala as the guests of honour. It's on Sunday in Fairyland – will you come?"

She gazed at them with eager eyes, and the girls clasped each other's hands in excitement.

"Guests of honour?" Kirsty repeated. "We'd love to come – but why us?"

"Because you have helped Fairyland so many times," said Elsa, opening her arms. "As soon as the king and queen asked me to organise the gala, I thought of you. They were delighted to agree."

"Thank you so much!" said Rachel. "Shall we use our lockets to travel to the Fairyland Palace?"

Queen Titania had given each of them a locket containing enough fairy dust to bring them to Fairyland. But Elsa shook her head.

"You will be magically brought to Fairyland at seven o'clock on Sunday evening," she said.

"I can hardly wait!" said Kirsty.

"I can't wait," said Rachel, hopping from one foot to the other.

Elsa laughed. "Would you like to come now and help with the preparations?" she asked.

The girls hugged each other, jumped and down, squealed and then hugged again.

"I think that's a yes!" said Elsa.

She glanced around to check that no one was watching, and then waved her wand. A thin, silvery ribbon whirled around the girls and whisked them into the air beside Elsa, shrinking them to fairy size. Wings as delicate as snowflakes unfolded on their backs, and a sprig of mistletoe floated down from the stall to hover between them. Elsa's wand danced above it, coiling it into the shape of a carriage with mistletoe-berry wheels and mistletoe-leaf seats.

The snow was falling even more thickly now, hiding them from the sight of any curious human eyes. Elsa tapped one of the carriage doors with her wand, and it opened at once.

"Please, climb in," she said.

The leaf seats were soft and springy, and changed to fit their shape when they sat down. As soon as they were ready, the carriage lifted them high into the winter sky and whisked them away. They tried to look out of the window, but all they could see were the swirling flakes of snow. Then there was a change in the light outside, the carriage sank downwards, and the door flew open. They had arrived at the Fairyland Palace.

"Welcome!" called a friendly voice.

Rachel and Kirsty stepped out of the carriage and saw Bertram the Frog Footman smiling at them from the doorway of the palace.

"Hello, Bertram!" called Rachel. "How are you?"

"All the better for seeing you," Bertram replied with a bow.

"The gala is being held in the ballroom," said Elsa, linking her arms through theirs. "Let's go and see how the decorating is going!"

Rachel and Kirsty paused in the doorway of the ballroom, smiling. Their friends the Showtime Fairies were fluttering around the room, draping garlands of holly, tinsel and mistletoe from corner to corner and against the walls. Silver trays were floating from fairy to fairy, carrying goblets of delicious-smelling drinks and snowman- and reindeer-shaped gingerbread. The merry chatter and laughter of the fairies made the room seem twice as full.

"Rachel! Kirsty!" cried Leah the Theatre Fairy, spotting them.

The seven fairies zoomed towards them and pulled them into a big hug.

"We're here to help Elsa prepare for the gala," said Darcey the Dance Diva Fairy. "We didn't know that you'd be here. What a lovely surprise!"

"It's a lovely surprise for us, too," said Kirsty, gazing up at the fancy decorations. "It looks as if the gala is going to be a spectacular event!"

"There will be special performances and lots of dancing," said Elsa. "Even Jack Frost is here to watch the preparations and enjoy a Christmassy glass of mulled blackcurrant cordial."

To their surprise, the girls saw that Jack Frost was indeed sitting on a golden chair in the corner. His cloak was wrapped tightly around him, and his spiky head was bowed over a plate of gingerbread.

"It's not like him to be so quiet," Rachel whispered to Kirsty as the Showtime Fairies flew off to carry on with the decorating.

"I can't see his face, but I bet he's looking grumpy," Kirsty whispered back. "He never likes to see the fairies having fun."

Just then, they heard raised voices from the other side of the ballroom.

"Red!" Taylor the Talent Show Fairy snapped at Madison the Magic Show Fairy. "It has to be red!"

"Silver tinsel would look much prettier on the tables," Madison argued, her hands on her hips. "Don't you have any taste?"

Leah pulled a foil chain down from the ceiling, frowning at Darcey.

"You've hung it all wrong!" she complained.

Suddenly the whole ballroom was filled with the sound of bickering fairies. Rachel, Kirsty and Elsa stared at the Showtime Fairies.

"What is wrong with everyone?" Elsa asked in confusion.

There was a commotion in the hall outside the ballroom, and then Holly the Christmas Fairy zoomed in and darted to

Elsa's side, taking her hand.

"Elsa, I'm afraid I've got some bad news," she said. "There's been a robbery in Holly Berry Lane. All three of your magical objects have been stolen!"

Looking horrified, Elsa sank into a nearby chair. Rachel and Kirsty stared at Holly in shock.

"What's Holly Berry Lane?" Kirsty asked.

"It's the home of all the fairies who help look after Christmas," Holly explained. "Elsa, I'm sure that Rachel and Kirsty will have an idea that will help."

But Elsa didn't seem to be listening. She was staring into space.

"How am I going to organise the Christmas Gala?" she asked. "How can I keep everyone happy in the human world without my magical objects?"

Rachel put her arm around Elsa's shoulders.

"Tell us about your magical objects," she said in a gentle voice.

Read **Elsa the Mistletoe Fairy** to find out what adventures are in store for Kirsty and Rachel!

RAINBOW magic

Calling all parents, carers and teachers!
The Rainbow Magic fairies are here to help
your child enter the magical world of reading.
Whatever reading stage they are at, there's
a Rainbow Magic book for everyone!
Here is Lydia the Reading Fairy's guide to
supporting your child's journey at all levels.

Starting Out

Our Rainbow Magic Beginner Readers are perfect for first-time readers who are just beginning to develop reading skills and confidence. Approved by teachers, they contain a full range of educational levelling, as well as lively full-colour illustrations.

1

Developing Readers

Rainbow Magic Early Readers contain longer stories and wider vocabulary for building stamina and growing confidence. These are adaptations of our most popular Rainbow Magic stories, specially developed for younger readers in conjunction with an Early Years reading consultant, with full-colour illustrations.

2

Going Solo

The Rainbow Magic chapter books - a mixture of series and one-off specials - contain accessible writing to encourage your child to venture into reading independently. These highly collectible and much-loved magical stories inspire a love of reading to last a lifetime.

3

www.rainbowmagicbooks.co.uk

"Rainbow Magic got my daughter reading chapter books. Great sparkly covers, cute fairies and traditional stories full of magic that she found impossible to put down" - Mother of Edie (6 years)

"Florence LOVES the Rainbow Magic books. She really enjoys reading now" Mother of Florence (6 years)

The Rainbow Magic Reading Challenge

Well done, fairy friend – you have completed the book!
This book was worth 10 points.

See how far you have climbed on the
Reading Rainbow opposite.

The more books you read, the more points you will get,
and the closer you will be to becoming a Fairy Princess!

Do you want your own Reading Rainbow?
1. Cut out the coin below
2. Go to the Rainbow Magic website
3. Download and print out your poster
4. Add your coin and climb up the Reading Rainbow!

There's all this and lots more at
www.rainbowmagicbooks.co.uk

You'll find activities, competitions, stories, a special
newsletter and complete profiles of all the
Rainbow Magic fairies. Find a fairy with your name!